NIGHT-TIME NUMBERS

A SCARY COUNTING BOOK

45

NIGHT-TIME NUMBERS

A SCARY COUNTING BOOK

SCHOLASTIC INC.
New York Toronto London Auckland Sydney
Mexico City New Delhi Hong Kong

ISBN 0-439-14555-4

Published by Scholastic Inc., 555 Broadway, New York, NY 10012,
by arrangement with Barefoot Books.

12 11 10 9 8 7 6 5 4 3 2 1 9/9 0 1 2 3 4/0

Printed in the U.S.A. 08

First Scholastic printing, October 1999

Font design by Susan L. Roth and Robert Salazar
The collages in this book were created from papers and fabrics collected by Susan L. Roth from all over the earth and moon.

Who can you see in
the backyard tonight?

I can see
one monster
in the pale
moonlight.
1

Who can you see in
the doorway tonight?

2 I can see two dragons in the pale moonlight.

Who can you see at
the window tonight?

I can see three
witches in the
pale moonlight.
3

Who can you see on
the staircase tonight?

I can see four skeletons
in the pale moonlight.

Who can you see in
the corner tonight?

5
I can see
five wolves
in the pale
moonlight.

Who can you see in
the bath-tub tonight?

6

I can see six sharks in the pale moonlight.

Who can you see in
the toy chest tonight?

I can see seven spiders in the pale moonlight.

7

Who can you see in
the closet tonight?

I can see eight ghosts in the pale moonlight.

Who can you see by
the chimney tonight?

I can see nine goblins
in the pale moonlight.

Who can you see on
the rooftops tonight?

10
I can see
ten bats
in the pale
moonlight.

Who can you see
shining all around?

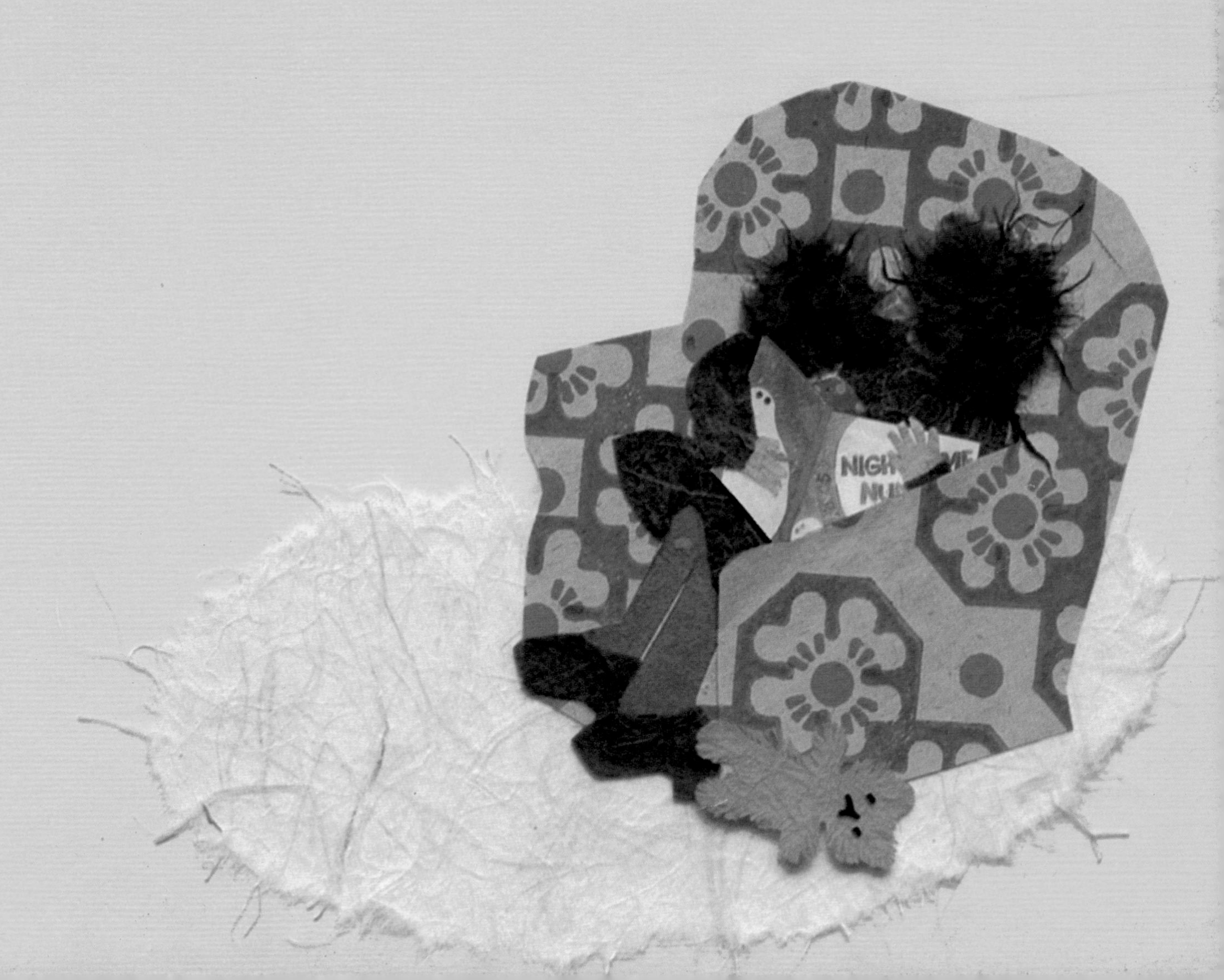

I can see an
angel, to keep me
safe and sound.

678